Abby's First Day of School!

MAKING THE MOST OF JR. CINE-MANGA®

Books use lots of creative techniques to tell stories. The speech balloons and sound effects in comic-style stories are an exciting way for your child to experience the printed word. Here's how you can make the experience even more interactive and playful:

- The first pages introduce the characters and the story. Point to the portraits as you name Abby and her friends. When you revisit the book, ask your child to tell you who everyone is as you point to their labels and ask what they think the story will be about.

- As you read aloud, point to the words in the speech balloons and other words on the page. As you return to the stories, you'll find that kids will "read" some of the words along with you, especially the sound effects. Pages should be read from top to bottom, first the left-hand page, then the right.

- Change your voice from character to character. You don't have to match Abby's funny tones exactly...kids will get a kick out of any goofy voices you put on.

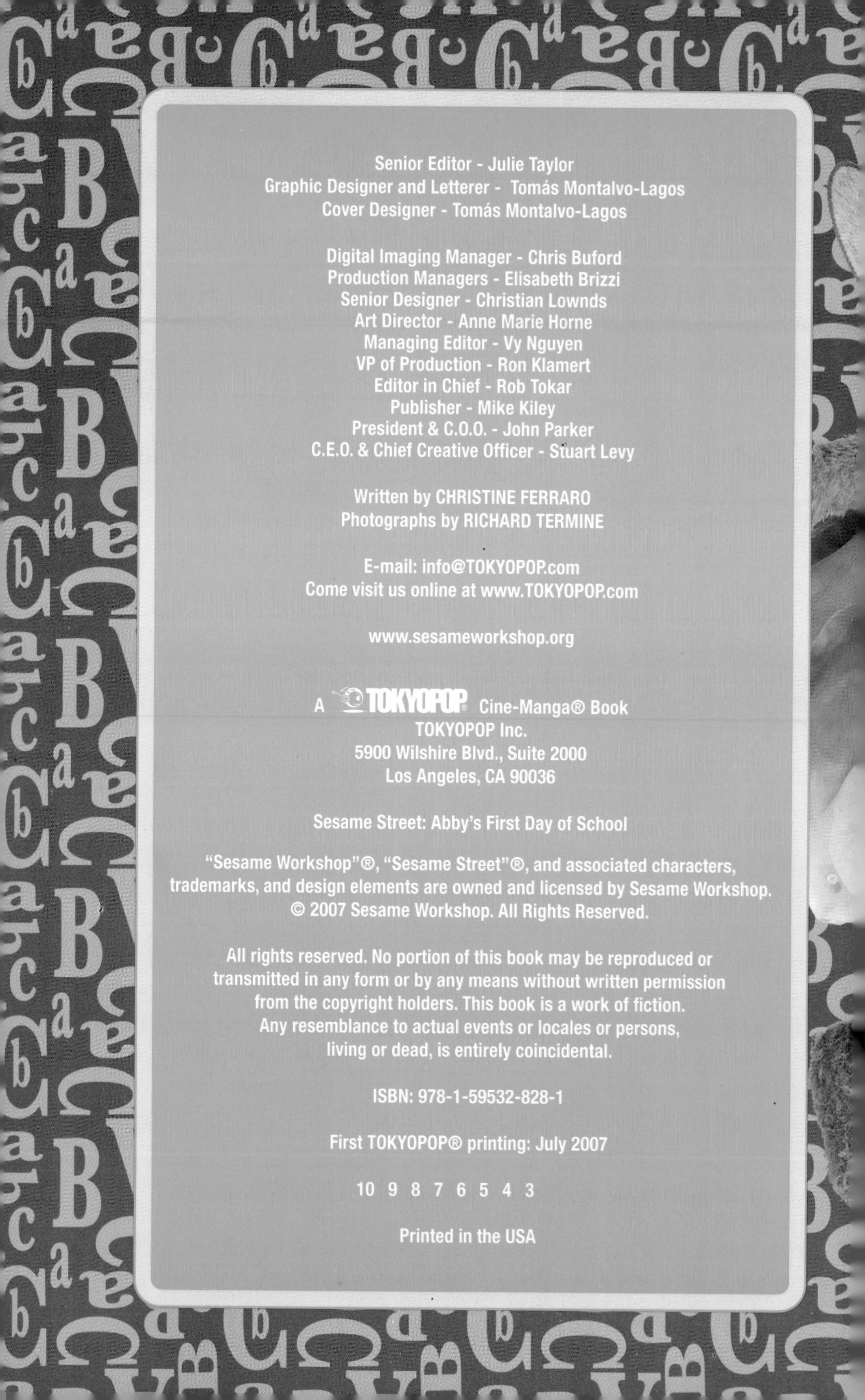

Senior Editor - Julie Taylor
Graphic Designer and Letterer - Tomás Montalvo-Lagos
Cover Designer - Tomás Montalvo-Lagos

Digital Imaging Manager - Chris Buford
Production Managers - Elisabeth Brizzi
Senior Designer - Christian Lownds
Art Director - Anne Marie Horne
Managing Editor - Vy Nguyen
VP of Production - Ron Klamert
Editor in Chief - Rob Tokar
Publisher - Mike Kiley
President & C.O.O. - John Parker
C.E.O. & Chief Creative Officer - Stuart Levy

Written by CHRISTINE FERRARO
Photographs by RICHARD TERMINE

E-mail: info@TOKYOPOP.com
Come visit us online at www.TOKYOPOP.com

www.sesameworkshop.org

A TOKYOPOP Cine-Manga® Book
TOKYOPOP Inc.
5900 Wilshire Blvd., Suite 2000
Los Angeles, CA 90036

Sesame Street: Abby's First Day of School

ISBN: 978-1-59532-828-1

First TOKYOPOP® printing: July 2007

10 9 8 7 6 5 4 3

Printed in the USA

Abby's First Day of School!
TOKYOPOP
HAMBURG · LONDON · LOS ANGELES · TOKYO

ABBY'S FIRST DAY OF SCHOOL WAS AN EXCITING DAY ON SESAME STREET. SHE AND ELMO CAN'T WAIT TO TELL YOU ALL ABOUT IT.

Elmo's friend Abby loves school!

Remember, Elmo? I kept poofing back and forth!

IT ALL BEGAN WHEN BABY BEAR WENT LOOKING FOR ABBY…
Hey, have you seen Abby Cadabby?
Abby? No.
Haven't seen her.

OP
We're supposed to go to school together. It's her first day!
SE
HABLA
SPAÑOL
ABBY AND BABY BEAR WERE GOING TO STORYBOOK COMMUNITY SCHOOL.

That's the perfect place for a fairy goddaughter like Abby!

POOF!
Where am I?
Oh, I'm here!
OPE
I'm ready, I'm ready, I'm ready!! Let's go to school!

ELMO WAS FEELING A LITTLE LEFT OUT. HE WISHED HE WAS GOING TO SCHOOL, TOO.
Will Abby tell Elmo everything that happens?
I will! I promise!

STORYBOOK COMMUNITY SCHOOL
LOOK WHO WAS WAITING AT THE STORYBOOK COMMUNITY SCHOOL. IT WAS ABBY'S TEACHER, MRS. GOOSE.
Otherwise known as Mother Goose!
I love my teacher! Do YOU know any Mother Goose stories?
Hello, Abby! You know, I taught your mother once upon a time...

...before she was Cinderella's Fairy Godmother.
Oh, Mrs. Mother Goose, ma'am...I...I...I want to learn everything!

Let's meet some of your classmates...
We're Jack and Jill...
...the ones who climbed that hill.

I'm Peter Piper, the pickled pepper picker!
He sure likes the letter P.
"Peter Piper Picked a Peck of Pickled Peppers." That tickles Elmo's tongue!
And here's Mary and her little lamb.

Hello!
I am Hansel.
And I am
Gretel.
And I am
Little Red
Riding Hood.
Elmo loves
the stories of
Little Red Ridin
Hood and Hanse
and Gretel. Ask
someone to tel
them to you!

Welcome, Abby!
Wow!
This place is so
amazing!

ABBY TOUCHED HER WAND TO HER HEAD AND...POOF!
Mrs. Goose
3 sides
4 sides
3
+ 4
7

SHE DISAPPEARED.
TWINK!

Mrs. Goose
Huh?
Where'd she go?

MEANWHILE, IN FRONT OF THE FIX-IT SHOP...
POOF!
Elmo!
Elmo!
Elmo!

Wait - what is Abby doing here?
ABBY WAS SOOOO EXCITED! SHE TOLD ELMO ALL ABOUT SCHOOL SO FAR.
...And Mother Goose is the teacher! I'll tell you more later, Elmo! Bye!

POOF!
IN A TWINKLING, ABBY WAS BACK IN CLASS.
Sorry I disappeared. I had to tell Elmo all about this place!

IT WAS A GOOD THING THAT ABBY CAME BACK. SHE'D ALMOST MISSED SHOW-AND-TELL!
I want to show you a new trick that Lamby has learned.
He can sound like other animals!
MOOOO!

Can anyone guess what animal that was? Anyone? Anyone?
Can YOU guess? Elmo knows!

A cow!
OINK! OINK!
Do you know this one?

I'm pretty positive that's a pig.
NEIGH! NEIGH!
Which animal is this?

If I'm not mistaken, that would be...a horse.
Exactly!
Take a bow, Lamby!

MOTHER GOOSE INVITED ABBY TO JOIN IN SHOW-AND-TELL...
If only I had brought something interesting that I could show you!

Maybe the answer is right at your fingertips...?
My wand!
I can use it to go ask Elmo for help!

ABBY DISAPPEARED...
TWINK!
BACK ON SESAME STREET, ABBY SHARED HER PROBLEM WITH ELMO.
POOF!
I really, really want to show them something interesting!

Elmo had a great idea! Elmo told Abby to show everyone her WAND.
Elmo loves when Abby taps her wand on her head like this and -
TWINK!

BACK AT SCHOOL, ABBY'S CLASS WAS IN FOR A SURPRISE...
POOF!

Elmo?! What are YOU doing here?
Where is Elmo...?

POOF!
THEN GUESS WHO ELSE POPPED IN!

Abby!

Mrs. Goose, guess what? I can do show-and-tell now! I've got the perfect thing!
U
X E
I want to show Elmo to everybody and tell them... he's my friend!
U
X E
Did you like our story?
THE END!